Dear Bryan.
Have a very
Happy Birthday
Lots of Love

Mrs. Hope &
all the children
at the Day care.

We Love very
you very
& much.

July. 1985.
3rd Birthday

Our Three Friends Who Saved the Day?

Illustrated by J.-L. Macias S.

Fall is almost over. Soon it will be winter and the countryside will be covered with snow. Daniel, Pamela and Nancy have decided to go fishing. They are going to the nearby river with some friends. Daniel is very proud of his new fishing rod. "We don't need to bring anything to eat," he says. "We'll catch enough fish to feed everyone."

The children arrive at the fishing spot opposite the tiny cottage where John the forester lives. John and his dog have come out to greet them. "You are here on a good fishing day," he tells them. "It rained very hard last night, and by tomorrow the muddy water will have run down the river and the fish will hide away under the rocks."

They catch lots of fish. Cliff decides to cook the fish himself. "You see, Pamela," he says proudly, "there are enough fish for all of us." Everyone is happy, but David notices that the old forester and his dog are staring up at the mountain.

Suddenly the woods become silent. The dog senses danger, but what can it be? Everything is too quiet. The birds have stopped singing . . . not a sound is heard. All of the wild animals have disappeared. One little squirrel hurries past as fast as he can. What is happening?

Then the scary silence in the forest changes to a terrifying noise of broken branches, and suddenly a torrent of water rushes down the mountain. It is the rain water from last night which has been trapped in a dam of fallen branches and stones, and now everything is breaking loose.

It all happens so fast. The muddy water rushes toward the river. "Quick, children!" cries the old forester. "The water will rise dangerously!" Everyone runs for safety up the mountain, except for Nancy and one little boy. They are in a boat which is being carried away by the river's current. "Help!" cries Nancy. "I must get to them before they reach the rapids!" Daniel shouts as he quickly jumps on his horse.

Daniel hurriedly gallops on his horse, but he can't catch up with the boat. The current is getting swifter and it is carrying the little boat toward the dangerous rapids.

It seems too late to help. But then suddenly a big brown bear appears on a tree trunk that has fallen into the river. Nancy recognizes him and cries "Cuddles! Cuddles! Help! Help!"

In a few moments the bear gently picks up the children in his paws and brings them to safety just as the little boat is pulled wildly down the river by the current.

Daniel watches anxiously from a distance. Nancy, so happy that she and her little friend have been rescued, runs toward her brother crying, "You saw what happened, didn't you? Cuddles saved us both!"

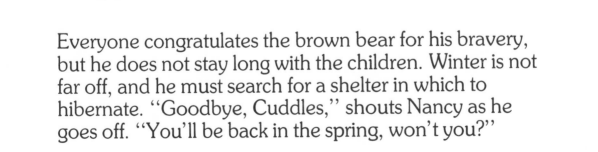

Everyone congratulates the brown bear for his bravery,
but he does not stay long with the children. Winter is not
far off, and he must search for a shelter in which to
hibernate. "Goodbye, Cuddles," shouts Nancy as he
goes off. "You'll be back in the spring, won't you?"

Published in the United States and simultaneously in Canada by Joshua Morris, Inc
431 Post Road East, Westport, CT.06880
Printed in Belgium